Ginny Morris and Mom's House Dad's House

For Kim, Patrick, Katy, and Shannon,
and for the children who inspire me every day
with their spirit, courage, and good humor — MCG

Published by
MAGINATION PRESS
An Educational Publishing Foundation Book
American Psychological Association
750 First Street, NE
Washington, DC 20002

For more information about our books, including a complete catalog, please write to us,
call 1-800-374-2721, or visit our website at www.maginationpress.com.

Editor: Darcie Conner Johnston
Art Director: Susan K. White
The text type is New Baskerville
Printed by Worzalla, Stevens Point, Wisconsin

Library of Congress Cataloging-in-Publication Data

Gallagher, Mary Collins.
Ginny Morris and Mom's house, Dad's house / by Mary Collins Gallagher ;
illustrated by Whitney Martin.
p. cm.
"An Educational Publishing Foundation Book."
Summary: Two years after her parents' divorce,
almost-nine-year-old Ginny Morris is still frustrated by trying to keep track of
clothing and homework as she moves from one house to another each Sunday,
but is learning to tell her parents when things bother her.
ISBN 1-59147-157-5 (hardcover : alk. paper) — ISBN 1-59147-158-3 (pbk. : alk. paper)
[1. Custody of children—Fiction. 2. Divorce—Fiction. 3. Schools—Fiction.]
I. Martin, Whitney, 1968- ill. II. Title.
PZ7.G13617Gi 2005
[Fic]—dc22 2004000953

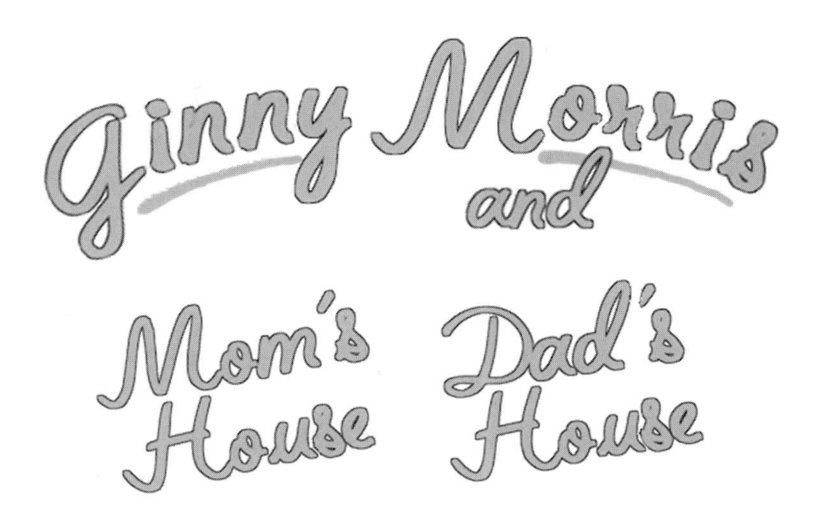

written by Mary Collins Gallagher

illustrated by Whitney Martin

MAGINATION PRESS • WASHINGTON, DC

Dear Reader,

Life is complicated. That's a fact. And it can seem twice as complicated when your parents are divorced or separated, and you live with each of them, but not at the same time. If you are like Ginny Morris and have two homes, you may understand the feelings she has about dividing her life between her parents. And you may also understand the trouble she gets herself into in *Ginny Morris and Mom's House, Dad's House.*

Ginny may not be the most organized kid in the world. But hey, it's really hard keeping track of things—like homework and gym shoes—especially when she has to take them back and forth between her mom's apartment and her dad's house. And it doesn't help that her fourth-grade teacher isn't sympathetic when she forgets her homework, or that she has to borrow sneakers with pink laces from the lost and found!

To add to the confusion, Ginny's parents have different rules, different ways of doing things. That's often the case with divorced parents. Kids can sometimes feel like they are living two separate lives, or as Ginny views it, two half lives.

And finally, kids who live in two homes usually have a hard time saying goodbye to a parent, a pet, neighborhood friends, an activity—even though they are happy to go to their other home and be with their other parent. Ginny does find ways to stay connected to both parents and to her friends when she can't be with them. Still, there are times when she wishes that her mom and dad would get back together, or that she lived with just one of them so she could stay in one place.

For the most part, kids don't get a say in the BIG decisions their parents make, like whether to divorce and where the children will live. But there are lots of things kids can control and there are lots of ways to feel better about the things they can't. I invite you into Ginny's world where she figures things out, often with humor and spunk, and she decides that her family is "still the best, even in halves."

Take care,
Mary Collins Gallagher

Chapter 1

My name is Ginny Morris. I live at 1170 Birdie Ave. Apartment 3C with my mom, and at 385 Knickerbocker Rd. with my dad. I have two bedrooms. Each one is filled with half my clothes, half my books and art stuff, half my rock collection. It's been this way since they got divorced two years ago. The judge called it joint custody. It means Mom and Dad both take care of me, just not at the same time. Dad got custody of Charlie, our cat. Mom got our dog, Daisy. It's sad, if you ask me, that Charlie and Daisy had to split up. They liked each other.

Today is Sunday, switch day, the day I leave one parent and go live with the other one for a week. Mom and I started out like we do most switch days, with bagels at Zingerman's—cinnamon for me, raisin with cream cheese for her. We read one more chapter of *Tuck Everlasting* and then took Daisy for a walk.

After that, Aunt Lindsey, Uncle Bruce, and my five-year-old twin cousins came down from 6B to say goodbye and to hear me play "When the Saints Go Marching In." I can play it all the way through without stopping on the keyboard that we got at a garage sale last summer. I take piano lessons from Mrs. Winters in 1B.

Tasha and Mitchell begged me to play puppies with them before I went to Dad's. Puppies is the same as house, only we're dogs instead of people. I said okay. I wouldn't have to play their baby games for a week.

I packed my journal, my homework folder, my best jeans, and my gym shoes. I put Leroy on top and held him down so he wouldn't get caught in the zipper. He's been patched up a few times already. One of these days I'll leave Leroy at Mom's or Dad's, but not today. I don't care if it is babyish for a fourth grader to sleep with a stuffed monkey.

I let Daisy lick my whole face—I always do before I leave. Then Mom drove me to Dad's house and gave me a long hug. Before I got out of the car we shook pinkies—it's how we say goodbye.

"Ginny!" Dad said, and squeezed me hard. "How about riding bikes to the park?"

That's what we usually do when I get to his house on switch days. Bike riding helps me with the lonely feeling that comes when I know I won't see my mom for a whole week.

Chapter 2

"Ginny, you'll miss your bus."

"I can't find my shoe!"

"Wear some other ones!"

The bus lights were flashing. I jogged down the sidewalk as fast as I could in sandals. Rebecca—she's my best friend—stood on the curb waving and yelling for me to hurry up. "What took you so long?" she said, climbing up the bus steps.

"I couldn't find one of my gym shoes." We looked at my feet.

"You can't play soccer in those."

"I know."

"Did you leave it at your mom's?"

"Or someone stole it while I was sleeping."

"Probably a robber," she said.

A man with a mustache and a ponytail was sitting in the driver's seat. He held a clipboard and was checking off names as kids walked past him.

"Who's that? Where's Ms. Peet?" I said. "Is this our bus?"

"That's Mr. Bilby. I forgot to tell you, we have him now. He made us have a seating chart. If you were here we could have picked each other to sit by."

The new bus driver looked real hard at me. "Are you new?" he said.

"No, but I don't take the bus all the time. My mom drives me to school every other week."

"Every other week, huh?" he said, tapping his pencil on the clipboard. "My name's Mr. Bilby. What's yours?"

"Ginny Morris."

I scanned the rows of seats. Kids were in the wrong places. Rebecca was way in the back with Marina Lewis instead of with me in the middle, where fourth graders are supposed to sit.

"Ginny, you can take a seat up front here next to Dominic. He's new, too."

"But I'm not new," I grumbled to myself and plopped down. How could everything change so much in one week? I did feel like a new kid.

My throat felt blocked up. My face was hot. Oh, no—my eyes were getting watery. I couldn't cry. I bent down, pretending I dropped something, and wiped my eyes with my shirt. I glanced at the new kid. His forehead was pressed against the window. "Is this your first day?" I asked him.

He looked my way. "Yeah." His voice was raspy, and his eyebrows were pinched together like he was concentrating, maybe on not crying, like I was.

"Who's your teacher?" I asked.

"I don't know yet." He seemed to be having trouble swallowing, too.

"What grade?"

"Fourth," he said, and stared out the window.

I didn't feel much like talking either.

When the bus came to a squeaky stop in front of the

school, Mr. Bilby swiveled toward me and the new kid.

"Ginny? How about showing Dominic around and taking him to the office so he can get settled?"

Rebecca must have heard because she was by my side in a second, volunteering to help. Dominic shrugged and followed us into the building.

I don't know what it is about new kids, but everyone always wants them in their class, even if they don't talk much, like this one didn't. Since there are three fourth-grade classrooms, there was a pretty good chance he'd be in my room or in Rebecca's. That's two out of three. Back on the first day of school, Rebecca and I got the bad news that we weren't in the same class—again. We haven't been together since second grade.

But the secretary said Dominic was in Mr. Julius's room. That meant neither one of us got him.

We gave him a little tour and dropped him off at his classroom door. "See you on the bus," I called to him, but he didn't say anything back. We watched him walk over to Mr. Julius's desk, looking really shy.

"Was he that quiet on the bus?"

"Yeah, he was." I sighed. "I wish I could sit with you, Rebecca."

"Me too."

The tardy buzzer went off.

Chapter 3

Ms. Riley gave me a "you're late but we'll ignore it this time" look when I speed-walked through the door. She was collecting our book reports. It was the first one we had to do this year. I did mine on *The Great Gilly Hopkins*, by Katherine Paterson. That was one of the best books I ever read. It was sad and funny. Gilly didn't get to live with either one of her parents.

I opened my homework folder, and let out a silent scream. The folder was as empty as the day I got it! I rushed to the coatroom and checked my backpack: lunch bag, four pennies, a soccer ball shaped eraser, and a broken pencil, but that was it. This was only the third week of fourth grade, and I didn't know what Ms. Riley would do. She didn't seem like a yeller, but adults can surprise you. I decided to get it over with.

“Ms. Riley? I did my book report, but now I can’t find it.” My mouth felt like it was full of chalk dust. “I think maybe I left it at my mom’s apartment. You can even call her. She was a witness to me doing it, and....” I stopped trying to explain when I saw Ms. Riley’s eyes get narrow.

“Ginny, this is fourth grade. You are responsible for doing your homework and for turning it in on time.” She was serious.

“I know,” I said, barely above a whisper. My mouth had gotten too dry and dusty to say it any louder.

“If you did it, you should be able to rewrite it without too much difficulty—at recess,” she said, and patted my shoulder like she felt sorry for me, like it had been a different mean teacher who just told me I had to stay in for recess.

Chapter 4

Charlie meowed and rubbed up against my legs when I got home. Mrs. Howard—she's a lady who lives across the street—sat on the couch watching TV. I told Dad I didn't need a babysitter. He said he'd think about it—in another three years.

"Hi, Mrs. Howard."

"Hello, dear," she said and patted the cushion next to her, inviting me to sit down. She was all engrossed in her favorite soap opera. When the commercial came on, she looked at me and smiled. "How was your day?"

"Okay."

"Homework?"

"A little." I got up and headed to my room.

Mrs. Howard made a noise like she was choking. The first time she did that, I was ready to slap her on her back or call an ambulance. Now I'm used to it. It's just her getting excited about what's happening on her show.

I fumbled through my rumpled up sheets and blankets looking for my journal. I wanted to write a letter to Grammy, like I do whenever I need to talk about things on my mind. I can never send the letters to her, and she will definitely never write back, because she died last year. But I write to her anyway because thinking about her makes it easy to put down what I feel, and that helps.

She was my great grandma Virginia. I was named after her. "Tell me about your week," she would say, and I'd let it all out. I told her the hard things, like what it was like when Mom and Dad separated, and about living in two places. She wanted to hear about other things, too, like soccer games, fights with my friends, and regular stuff, even the kind of breakfast cereal I ate. She'd squeeze my hand, nod, and talk just a little. I miss her a lot, but writing to her makes me feel like she's still here in a way.

Dear Grammy,

I felt like I landed on another planet when I got on the bus today. I didn't feel like I belonged. Rebecca said she'd tell me if any other weird stuff happens when I'm at Mom's. I hope she doesn't forget. The new kid must have felt worse than I did. His name is Dominic. It's scary when you don't know what's going to happen. Even when you're pretty sure things will be okay, it's hard to relax until they are. On the way home Dominic said he didn't want to move to a new house or go to a new school. He might not be that bad to sit by.

I thought I would love fourth grade. It's a lot harder this year to remember everything. I hope my shoe didn't fall out of the car. If it's at Mom's I won't be able to get it until Sunday. She doesn't like coming over here. And Dad doesn't want to go over there. They don't say so. They say it's my responsibility to remember. But if they forgot something and really needed it, they'd hop right in the car and get it. I wish I could drive. I miss Mom.

Ginny

I searched every place in the whole house I thought a shoe might end up. All I found were my soccer shoes (which I'll be needing soon), my old sneakers (which crunch my toes), and my best geode (which has been missing since third grade).

I only had one work sheet—math—and it looked pretty easy. I decided to get some fresh air. Rebecca's brother Carlton was outside, so I rode bikes with him until Dad came home. Rebecca had to stay in and do her homework. She said Ms. Amani was piling it on like they were in high school.

Chapter 5

Dad showed me how to make the best macaroni and cheese in the world, with all natural ingredients, of course. He won't let us eat anything that's not organic—and that means no preservatives or anything artificial.

"Dad, I wish you could hear me play the keyboard," I said between mouthfuls.

"I do, too."

"Mrs. Winters thinks I should take lessons every week. Maybe you could drive me over, and then you could hear me play—on her piano."

"You'll be too busy for extra piano lessons for awhile," he said, smiling. "Soccer sign-up came in the mail."

"Yes!" I got so excited a macaroni fell out of my mouth. "Am I on the Fireballs again?"

He gave me thumbs up, and suddenly leaned forward like he was about to fly right out of his chair.

I knew just what he was thinking.

"Race you to the backyard!"

We made a goal with garbage cans. Dad was goalie, and I practiced taking shots until he did his horrible two-finger, ear-busting whistle.

"What? What did I do?"

He pointed at his watch. "Bedtime."

"Come on, Dad, I'm just starting to get the ball past you. And I'm not tired."

"No arguing with the coach."

Sigh.

In my room, I turned on my computer to check email. I had one from Mom.

```
Hi Ginny!
I found your book report on your desk. Weren't
you supposed to hand that in? Sweet dreams. Daisy
and I miss you and love you.
Mom
```

It was 9:30. I clicked reply and hoped she wouldn't notice how late it was.

> Hi Mom,
> I can't find one of my gym shoes. I think it might be under my bed. If you find it would you pleeeaase bring it to me? I know it's my responsibility to remember things, but I've been thinking. Once in awhile, if it's an emergency, if I forget something or if something happens and I really need you to come over here—would you?
> Love,
> Ginny
>
> P.S. I had to do the book report over at recess. Ms. Riley is not understanding like Mr. Fessler was last year. I miss you.

I was about to climb in bed when I saw the math worksheet Changing Fractions into Decimals. I groaned so loud that Charlie—who was curled up on my pillow—opened his eyes just long enough to give me one of his "you are bothering the king" looks.

I glared back at him with one of my "you are spoiled rotten" looks. "Daisy would get up and try to help me," I said.

He circled around and picked another cozy spot.

"You're getting broccoli in your dish tomorrow," I said, and sat down at my desk again. Ugh. All I wanted to do was curl up with him. I could barely keep my eyes open, but I pictured Ms. Riley giving me one of her "this is fourth grade" looks and got my math done.

No thanks to Charlie.

Chapter 6

"Wake up, Ginny," Dad said, standing over me. "We're running a little late."

I felt like I'd been sleeping for about five minutes. And Charlie was sprawled all over Changing Fractions into Decimals like it was his own personal quilt. I pulled it out from under him. "Charlie!" The paper was wrinkled, and he had poked holes in it with his claws.

I slipped on my soccer shoes and bolted down the street. Dominic said hi when I fell into the seat next to him. He smelled like pancakes, which reminded me of the health nut bar in my backpack. I didn't have time for breakfast, so Dad told me to eat it on the bus. He said it tasted like granola.

"Yuck!" I said, and spit it into a piece of scrap paper. "That's the worst thing I ever tasted."

"What is it?" Dominic asked.

"It's a health nut bar. It tastes like dirt."

"Let's see it." He held up the wrapper and started reading the list of ingredients: "oats, soy protein, blanched almonds...."

He looked up at me with his eyes open wide. "Fish scales," he said, shaking his head. "No wonder."

"What?" I grabbed it from him and checked the label to make sure he was joking.

Dominic was grinning. He broke off a crumb and laid it on his tongue. "Ptue." Then he reached into his backpack and pulled out a baggie filled with Oreos. "Hungry?"

That's what I call a good breakfast.

I thought no one would notice I was wearing my soccer shoes. On top they looked like regular black Nikes. It was the clicking of the cleats that gave me away. Mr. Tackett—he's our school principal—was standing inside the front door, and he heard me clicking down the hall. "Miss Morris, what do you have on your feet?"

"Busted," Dominic whispered.

Mr. Tackett made me go to the office. The secretary said I would scratch up the floors if I wore cleats around the building. She took me to a storage closet filled with old kids' clothes and shoes. There was only one pair in my size, and they were glittery and had pink laces, kind of like Barbie shoes. She made me put them on.

Ms. Riley smiled when I came through the door. I thought that was nice. I smiled back. "Mr. Tackett said you'd be a little late," she said. Then she looked at my feet, and I am

99.9 percent sure I heard her giggle. This was not the time I wanted to find out my teacher had a sense of humor. "Mrs. LaSelle made me wear them!" I announced, but that didn't stop everyone from laughing.

Well, she got serious again when I handed my math in. It was my job, she told me, to keep my cat off my homework. I had to copy it over—at recess. I should have just worn my sandals today.

Dear Grammy,

It would be easier if the rules for doing homework were the same at Mom's and Dad's. But that will never happen. Maybe I will just have to make my own rules for doing it, if I ever want to have recess again. On the way home I told Dominic I wouldn't be on the bus next week. That's when I found out his parents are divorced, too. He goes to his dad's every other weekend.

Ginny

Chapter 7

I cleared off the kitchen table and sharpened a pencil. It took twenty minutes to do the Life Cycle of the Dwarf African Frog. After that, spelling and social studies took about another twenty minutes.

Dad got home just as I was putting the papers in my assignment folder.

"Homework all done?" he asked.

"Yep." I put the folder in my backpack, and put the backpack by the front door. "Dad, do you think you could ask me when you come home every day if I did my homework?"

"Sure thing, if you think it would help."

"I think it would. I hope it would." I sighed. "Reeeally hope it would."

Dad gave me one of his "should I ask?" looks.

I gave him one of my "nah, you don't need to know" looks and yawned.

After dinner Dad tried to get me to eat one of his health nut bars. He bought a whole box of them! "No thanks, one bite of a gross nut bar is enough for a lifetime," I told him.

Dad thought that was funny. Then he started eating one and making an "mmm" sound while he was chewing it. Gross.

Hi Ginny,
I have no idea where that shoe is, but I'll keep looking. Your question about bending the rules in emergencies sounds fair. I forget things once in awhile, too. But is a gym shoe really an emergency? Did you get your homework done?
Love you,
Mom
P.S. Tasha and Mitchell dropped off an invitation for their birthday party. Your birthday isn't long after theirs. Let's start planning. Do your homework!

Thanks, Mom. My shoe is probably in my room or maybe it's under the couch. I wonder if Daisy hid it somewhere. It IS an emergency! I had to wear shoes from the school storage closet — glittery

and pink ones — shoes Tasha would love. I got my homework done. Mom, I'm in fourth grade now. I don't think I need so many reminders to do my homework — maybe just one. Okay?
Love,
Ginny

P.S. Do I really have to go to a kindergarten party?

Dear Grammy,

I didn't say anything back to Mom about my birthday because I don't like thinking about it. It feels like a big rock is rolling around in my stomach whenever I do. I don't want two parties, one with Mom and one with Dad, like last year. I don't want to blow out nine candles twice and make the same wish twice. I don't want my birthday to be in halves like most things are. Besides, nine isn't an even number. It can't be cut in half.

Ginny

Chapter 8

It was switch day. Dad and I made our usual gigantic Sunday morning breakfast. I think he loads me up with organic food before I leave because he thinks I eat only junk food at Mom's. I took a teeny bite of a tofu sausage (disgusting!) and stuffed myself with blueberry pancakes.

Then I started packing. To make sure I wouldn't forget anything, I made a list of all the things I need to take. I'd already collected the really important stuff in a basket I call my Do Not Forget OR You'll Be Sorry for the Next Seven Days basket.

I had it all: homework, Leroy, journal, shin guards, sandals (in case I had to keep wearing them), the glitter shoes (I hoped I could take them back to the school office), and my gym shoe (my fingers were crossed the other one was somewhere at Mom's).

I didn't like using up my time making a boring list, but it was better than missing recess or getting stuck wearing Barbie shoes.

When I was done packing, Dad showed me some soccer strategies. My first game is on Saturday. It will be Mom's week, but I know Dad will be there. He never misses a game.

Rebecca and I and Ernie Popper and Carlton rode our bikes to the park. They wanted to play soccer, too. Ernie lives on our street. He's a sixth grader, like Carlton. To keep it even, Carlton and I played against Ernie and Rebecca. Rebecca is the best goalie on the Fireballs, and I was actually getting shots past her. I dribbled the ball down the field and faked that I was going to shoot. Instead, I passed to Carlton and he made the goal. We high-fived. Then I saw Dad's truck parked at the curb.

"Great play!" he said. "Just like we practiced. Ginny, it's time to go to your mom's."

"Let's go later, Dad. Mom won't care."

"I'm supposed to get you there by four o'clock. Get your bike. I'll put it in the back. Your backpack and duffel bag are in the truck."

I was mad about having to leave, so I sat in the truck with my arms folded over my chest.

"Ginny, I was thinking about your birthday. Should we do it like last year—one little party with your mom and another with me?"

I'm sure Dad thought bringing up my birthday would snap me out of my bad mood, but it didn't. It made me feel like I was going to throw up.

"No thanks."

"Really?" Dad seemed surprised. "Why not?"

"Nine isn't an even number. It can't be cut in half."

We stopped at a red light. Dad looked at me with his head

tilted until the light turned green. "I don't understand," he said. "That doesn't make sense."

"It does to me."

We were almost at Mom's.

"Well, let's talk about it again next week, okay?" he said. "Oh, and would you give this to your mom?" He handed me an envelope.

"What is it?"

"It's about soccer."

Chapter 9

A note inside the soccer envelope made Mom mad. She didn't say so, but I could tell because her mouth got puckery and she stared into space instead of asking me a bunch of questions about school.

After dinner, she went into her bedroom. I heard her talking on the phone to Dad, and that is very rare. I think they were arguing. It was about who should pay for soccer. She said something about piano lessons, too. Doesn't she know I have excellent hearing?

I went to my room and turned on the radio. I made a tent by putting my bedspread over my desk. I got my journal and a flashlight, and huddled inside with Daisy and Leroy.

Dear Grammy,

I got scared when I heard Mom on the phone with Dad. I'm afraid they will get into a big fight about me.

When I told Dad I didn't want two birthday parties, he looked at me like I was talking to him in a different language.

I was happy to see Mom today, but I didn't want to say goodbye to Rebecca or Dad or stop playing soccer. I don't like leaving in the middle of things. Now soccer and the bus and Dominic and Dad are over for a week, except for our game on Saturday.

I wonder if Mom will come, or if she will drop me off and pick me up after the game, like she did all last season.
I miss Dad.

Ginny

I pulled my covers down to go to bed. Yes! My shoe was tucked under my blanket. I dumped my duffel bag out on the floor, and the other one tumbled out. I set them side by side next to my bed. Together at last!

Chapter 10

Rebecca asked me and some of the Fireballs to come over after the game Saturday to grill hot dogs for lunch. Guess whose kindergarten birthday party is at the exact same time? Mom said it would be very nice of me to go to the twins' party. She said Aunt Lindsey and Uncle Bruce would appreciate it, and Tasha and Mitchell would be thrilled. When adults start saying "very nice" and "appreciate," you might as well give up. You know you'll have to do it.

So I told Mom it would also be very nice if she watched my soccer game. She said okay, but I could tell she didn't feel right about it because of Dad being there. I wanted to tell her that Dad doesn't have custody of soccer, I do. I can invite anyone I want. Then I got to thinking about it, and I wasn't sure it was such a good idea for her to go to the game either. It would be terrible if they started arguing, right there in front of everybody, about who should pay for soccer. But I couldn't un-invite her.

I tried to concentrate on how excited I was about the game. We got red shirts, and red is my favorite color, also perfect for a team called the Fireballs. My number was 11—my lucky number, I decided—and this was our first game in my new division for kids who are in fourth, fifth, and sixth grade.

But it was hard to concentrate on the good things when I didn't know what Mom and Dad would do or what they'd say to each other. The more I thought about it, the more it made me mad that they might embarrass me or that I'd be too worried to have fun or play a good game.

On Saturday when we drove up to the field, Dad was already there. He waved. If it had been only me, he would have sprinted right over, but it wasn't, and he walked toward us—really slow. He gave me a hug. I was nervous, but he nodded to Mom, and she nodded back. And I let out the breath I didn't know I was holding.

When I stopped being so jittery I got mad again. Why couldn't they be friends, or at least pretend to be—for just one hour? Kids have to be nice to people they don't like. Why is it different for parents? "I have to go warm up," I said, and left the two of them standing there not saying anything to each other.

During the game, Mom stood by her car instead of following the action up and down the field, like Dad did. It seemed kind of silly to me that she stayed so far away, and I got a little mad again. But then I felt a little sad too. Maybe this wasn't so easy for Mom either.

Chapter 11

Mom and I got tacos at the drive-thru and ate in the car so I could get to the twins' birthday on time.

"Honey, I really loved watching you play!" she said.

"You did?"

"Of course I did. Next time I'll get closer so I can see more of the action—especially Number 11. Those passes you made helped almost win the game!"

I was shocked—and so happy. She really had been watching. Then I remembered how she looked standing alone by the car. "Are you sure? About coming?"

Mom nodded in a big way and gave me one of her "that's a strange question" looks.

Well, I wasn't so sure, but I decided to go along with her anyway. I mean, why not? Getting all worried again wouldn't do anything except give me a stomachache. And it wouldn't change anything. And I wouldn't have fun. So if she comes, great, and if not, well, Dad's at every game.

Phew, it felt good getting that figured out.

"Thanks, Mom."

I was sorry about missing Rebecca's soccer barbecue, but I had to admit those kindergarteners were kind of funny. I think she would have gotten a kick out of them, too.

Tasha and Mitchell tackled me when I got there. "We're aliens," Mitchell said, jiggling the antennae he was wearing on his head.

"That explains a lot," I said. "Happy birthday, aliens."

The theme for Tasha and Mitchell's birthday was outer space, and Aunt Lindsey asked me to help the kids make antennae with Styrofoam balls and pipe cleaners. Most of them were finished in about five minutes, which left an hour and twenty-five minutes for them to run around the apartment pretending to be creatures from outer space.

We tried playing musical chairs, which Uncle Bruce called musical planets, but they kept having big pile-ups so Aunt Lindsey stopped the game. She said she didn't want any parents to have to pick their kids up at the hospital.

When it was time for cake, Uncle Bruce tried to get them settled down by following them around saying, "Okay, all you aliens, it's time to come down to earth."

"Stop saying that," Aunt Lindsey told him. "You're just stirring them up by reminding them that they're aliens. Isn't he, Ginny?"

I shrugged. I was not about to take sides. At first I thought they were getting into a fight. But they weren't fighting, they were laughing.

Finally everyone sat at the table and sang "Happy Birthday." Mitchell and Tasha had their own cakes and their own six candles to blow out. Aunt Lindsey and Uncle Bruce stood behind them looking really tired, but also really happy. They asked me to take a picture. When I peered through the camera at all of them smiling together, I felt that big rock rolling around in my stomach again.

Dear Grammy,

Sometimes I think everything would be easier if I lived with one parent most of the time and visited the other one once in awhile, like Dominic does. But which parent? It makes me even sadder when I think about being with one of them less than I already am. What I really wish is for all of us to be together, but that will never happen. I guess this is the next best thing, even though sometimes it really stinks. I wonder if Mom and Dad ever had fun like Aunt Lindsey and Uncle Bruce.

Ginny

Chapter 12

Mom and I went to a new Chinese restaurant for dinner. When the waiter took my order, I said, "Could you please make that without MSG?"

Mom had just taken a drink of water. It must have gone down the wrong pipe because she started coughing.

"No problem," the waiter said to me. He handed Mom a napkin.

"Thank you," I said, and patted Mom on the shoulder.

"How about you, Ma'am?"

Mom cleared her throat. "Uh, sure, please hold the MSG on mine, too." After he left, she leaned across the table and put her hands on mine. Her eyes were still watery from coughing. "MSG?"

"It's a preservative, monosodium gluta-something. Dad told me about it. You know how he is about preservatives."

"I remember," she said, smiling just a little.

"Mom, I know a lot about cooking." I suddenly thought of

a great idea. "Hey! I'm going to write a natural foods cookbook for kids."

"Really?"

"And when I sell it, I'll give you and Dad money. For soccer and shoes and another keyboard or even a piano."

"Honey, why would you think you had to give us money?"

I felt my face get hot. "Well...."

"You heard me on the phone with your dad."

I nodded.

"You were kind of loud."

Mom didn't say anything, and she got that look like she was thinking about something far away.

I didn't know what to say so I took a drink of water. When I put my glass down, she was looking at me with her little smile again.

"I hope we didn't scare you," she said. "Your dad and I are trying to work all kinds of things out, and sometimes we do it better than at other times."

I took a deep breath.

"I hate it when you fight, and Mom—I really hate it when I have to carry messages between you and Dad. Sometimes I just want to rip them up instead of giving them to you because they're always about me. And when they make you mad I feel like it's my fault."

"Honey, of course it's not your fault, but I can imagine it feels that way. You're right—you shouldn't have to be the messenger. I'm sure we can find other ways to communicate without involving you."

"Mom, that would be reeeally nice."

Mom laughed. But then she looked serious again. "And as for money, your dad and I are in charge of soccer and whatever else you need. Go ahead and write that cookbook. I'm sure that I could learn a lot from it."

This time I laughed.

"But Ginny, do it because you want to, not because you think you have to. We're the adults. You concentrate on being almost nine."

Then she got all smiley, like she had just remembered the best news in the world. "And speaking of being almost nine—let's talk about your birthday!"

I sighed. It made me tired thinking about having to explain it to her.

Dear Grammy,

I felt a lot better when I told Mom that I heard her arguing with Dad. It's too hard keeping things like that inside. Writing helps, but sometimes I need to talk about it. I told her about nine not being an even number. She didn't think it made sense either, but she went along with it. She said I could have just one party, if that would be better. I said no thanks to that, too. One party would mean that only one parent would be there.

I told Rebecca about no parties, too. She said I'm crazy to pass up double presents, double cakes, twice the friends, twice the fun. She's not divorced, so she doesn't know that what sounds like double parties really feels like half parties.

Ginny

Chapter 13

Switch day came fast this week. After bagels, Mom and I read two more chapters of *Tuck Everlasting*. I wanted to keep reading. Mom said she wouldn't mind if I took it to Dad's and read it with him. I didn't want to. If I did, Mom would miss the rest of the book, and Dad doesn't know how it started. But I did want to take my keyboard. I've been asking since we got it. I really wanted Dad to hear me play.

"The keyboard is too big and old to be hauled around," she said for the hundredth time.

"Mom, I thought you said the keyboard was mine."

"It is. But I'd like you to keep it here."

"If it's mine, I should be able to take it to Dad's."

Mom gave me one of her "sorry, but that's the way it is" looks.

I gave her one of my "you make me so mad" looks. I was thinking about stomping out of the room.

Her face got softer. "Ginny, I don't mean to make things

any harder for you. I'm sure it's frustrating for you to keep so many things separate."

"It is, Mom. Only I'm not the one keeping everything separate."

"That's true, you're not."

That made me just want to throw the stupid keyboard out the window.

"Mom, sometimes you and Dad drive me crazy! How am I supposed to know when something is mine and when it's not really? When do I get to be the boss of my own stuff? When I'm 30?"

"I'd say way before that, honey, 28 at the latest."

"Mom!"

"25?"

"MOM!"

"Okay, Ginny," she started to laugh. "Look, in the case of the keyboard, it has to stay here. If it got damaged, we probably wouldn't be able to fix it, and you'd have no piano anywhere. But I promise to give reasonable consideration to other requests to take things back and forth to your dad's, if you promise to keep track of them."

"Well, I am almost nine."

"Only 16 years to go till you're 25."

"**MOM!**"

But I wasn't angry anymore.

Chapter 14

It's not easy to carry a backpack and a box filled with forty brownies on the bus. But that's what I was doing. Rebecca and Carlton helped by making it thirty-eight.

"I didn't know it was your birthday," Dominic said.

"It's not till tomorrow. Want one?" I said and opened the box.

He held up a brownie and inspected it. "Did your dad make these?"

"Don't worry, no fish scales."

He took a bite. "Are you having a party?" he asked.

"Not this year. If I was, I would have invited you."

"Mine's in June. I don't know if I'll have one either. But if I do I'll invite you, too."

I offered one to Mr. Bilby, and he sucked it down in one bite. Then he grabbed his microphone. "Let's sing 'Happy Birthday' to Ginny," and everyone did.

After school, when I was getting off the bus, Mr. Bilby said, "We'll miss you next week."

I don't exactly know why, but I was glad that he would miss me.

Chapter 15

Today is Saturday, September 29th, and I'm at Dad's. The only thing different about today is that I was born on it nine years ago at exactly 5:42 a.m. I've been nine for almost six hours.

Mom and Dad said having no parties was fine as long as that's the way I really wanted it. I said it was. I said this year I'd make my own celebration my own way. Maybe next year I'll want to have one party, or two. Maybe I won't.

For lunch, I'm going to make my specialty pizza with French bread, two kinds of cheese, pepperoni, green peppers, and pineapple, if we have any. I'll see Rebecca at our soccer game this afternoon. Maybe I'll invite her to sleep over. Maybe I won't.

Dad came into the kitchen while I was lining up my ingredients on the counter.

"Let's ride bikes to the park," he said.

"Maybe later. I'm a little busy now." I was also feeling a little grouchy. I didn't tell him that, because I was trying to be in a good mood. After all, it was my birthday.

"You're quiet today. Do you miss your mom?"

"Yeah, guess I do."

I opened the refrigerator and moved some things around, pretending to look for pineapple.

When I closed the door, Dad was standing there tilting his head like he does when he's trying to figure me out.

"Hmmm. I'm thinking that this isn't the birthday you hoped for, is it, Ginny?"

I took a deep breath.

"Well…Dad, I know you and Mom love me, but you don't know how hard it can be to live in two places and not have both of you at the same time—especially on my birthday."

"Try me. I'll listen."

My eyes got blurry, which surprised me because I didn't

think I felt like crying. I think they were the kind of tears that come out with words that are hard to say. Now that I said them, and Dad was trying to understand, I felt better. I could tell I felt better because I was wondering what was in the big box in the closet.

"Could we get ice cream at the park?" I said. "The not organic kind?"

"Sure, birthday girl."

"Helmets!" I shouted. In a second I was on my bike following Dad down the street. He was singing "Happy Birthday to You" really loud.

It was embarrassing, so I slowed down a little.

Dad got in line at the Dairy Freeze. I found a table and watched a big family having a picnic.

"Someday when I get older," I said to Dad when he sat down, "I'll plan my own party and it will look like that. If you want to come, you might have to play musical chairs with people you're not used to being with anymore."

"You mean your mom."

"Yeah, and no fighting allowed."

"I know you'd like us all to be together."

"It would sure make my life easier."

I tasted my chocolate chip pecan cookie dough.

"But I'd never want a different family. We're the best. Even in halves."

About the Author

MARY COLLINS GALLAGHER, L.P.C., is a school counselor who has worked with hundreds of children before, during, and after divorce and through joint custody situations. She has three grown children and lives in Ann Arbor, Michigan, with her husband and dog, Annie, the real Daisy.

Acknowledgements
I wish to thank my astute writing friends—Sharon Blankenship, Elsa Bruno, Dawn Chalker, and Lisa Patrell—who are always ready to read another draft, and my amazing editor, Darcie Conner Johnston, for challenging and encouraging me. — *MCG*

About the Illustrator

WHITNEY MARTIN's illustrations have appeared in books, magazines, and catalogs, and he has worked on many animation projects, including Walt Disney movies. Before his career as an artist, he was a sergeant in the U.S. Marine Corps Reserves. Whitney now lives in Santa Fe, New Mexico, with his wife and two children.